**Sports Illustrated KIDS**

FOR THE RECORD

# THE ULTIMATE COLLECTION OF PRO BASEBALL RECORDS

BY ANTHONY WACHOLTZ

CAPSTONE PRESS
a capstone imprint

Sports Illustrated Kids For the Record is published by Capstone Press,
1710 Roe Crest Drive, North Mankato, Minnesota 56003.
www.capstonepub.com

SI Kids is a trademark of Time Inc. Used with permission.

The author dedicates this book to Richard Wacholtz (for his baseball sense)
and Curt Buhl (the biggest die-hard Twins fan he knows).

*Library of Congress Cataloging-in-Publication Data*
Wacholtz, Anthony.
  The ultimate collection of pro baseball records / by Anthony Wacholtz.
    p. cm.—(Sports illlustrated kids. For the record.)
  Includes index.
  ISBN 978-1-4296-8714-0 (library binding)
  ISBN 978-1-4296-9428-5 (paperback)
  1. Baseball—Records—United States—Juvenile literature. I. Title.
  GV877.W335 2013
  796.357'64—dc23                           2012016718

**Editorial Credits**
Catherine Neitge, managing editor; Gene Bentdahl, designer; Eric Gohl, media researcher;
        Eric Manske, production specialist


**Photo Credits**
AP Images: 45; Corbis: Bettmann, 4–5, 11b; Getty Images: *Sporting News*, 30b; Library of
Congress: 9, 10t, 10b, 11t, 12t, 12b, 13t, 13b, 14b, 17b, 18t, 18b, 21, 23t, 23b, 25, 26t, 26b, 28t,
28b, 33t, 34b, 35m, 35b, 43b, 54b, 58, 60, 61t; Newscom: Icon SMI/Robert Beck, 36, 49t, Icon
SMI/*Sporting News* Archives, 42, Icon SMI/William A Guerro, 47t; Shutterstock: nikkytok,
cover, Tomislav Forgo, back cover (ball), zimmytws, back cover (field); *Sports Illustrated*: Al
Tielemans, 2m, 57t, 57b, Andy Hayt, 55, Bob Rosato, 29b, 48t, Chuck Solomon, 8t, 46, Damian
Strohmeyer, 15, 39t, David E. Klutho, 27, 37t, Heinz Kluetmeier, 19t, 48b, Hy Peskin, 20, 53t,
John Biever, 2b, 8b, 53b, 59, John D. Hanlon, 19b, 50b, John G. Zimmerman, 2t, 24, 29t, 39b,
John Iacono, 3, 22, 31t, 32, 34t, 40, 43t, 44, 56, John W. McDonough, 31b, Manny Millan, 37b,
50t, Mark Kauffman, 17t, Richard Meek, 41b, 51, Robert Beck, 16b, 38, 54t, Simon Bruty, 47b,
Tony Triolo, 30t, 61b, V.J. Lovero, 6, 7b, 33b, 35t, 49b, Walter Iooss Jr., 7t, 14t, 16t, 41t, 52

Design Elements
Shutterstock: ArtyFree, fmua, ssuaphotos, Tomislav Forgo, zimmytws

Printed in the United States of America in North Mankato, Minnesota.
042012     006682CGF12

# TABLE OF
# CONTENTS

# A GAME OF NUMBERS

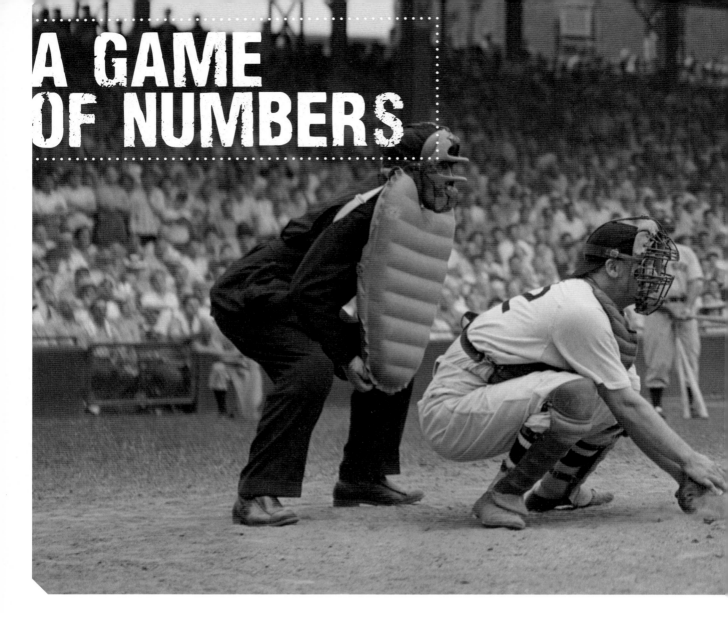

Joe DiMaggio stepped up to the plate for the New York Yankees on May 15, 1941. The cleanup hitter faced Eddie Smith of the Chicago White Sox. DiMaggio laced a single that would be his only hit of the day, and the Yankees lost 13-1. But the game would become a legendary piece of baseball history.

DiMaggio went on to collect at least one hit in game after game after game. He surpassed Willie Keeler's hit streak of 45 games from 1897. But he didn't stop there. He continued his streak until July 17. Facing the Cleveland Indians, DiMaggio went 0-3 with a walk. The remarkable streak ended at 56 games.

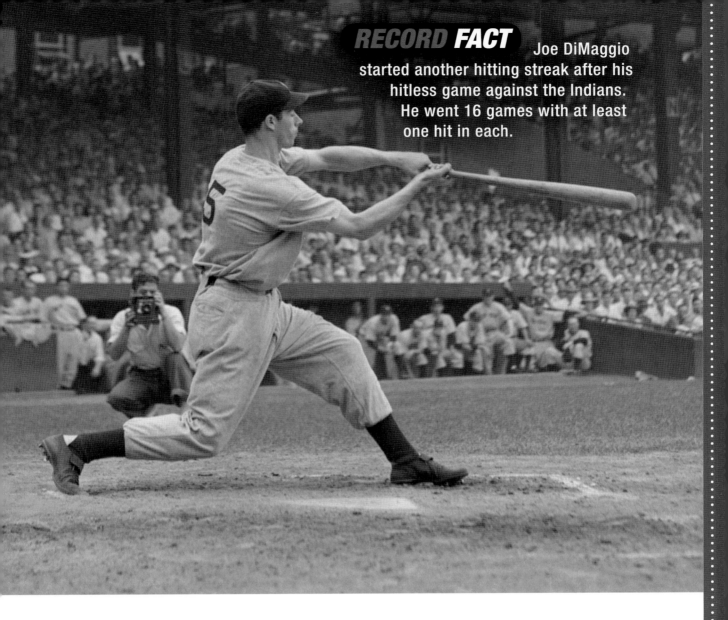

More than 70 years later, DiMaggio's streak is still intact. The only person to come close since DiMaggio set the record was the Cincinnati Reds' Pete Rose, who reached 44 games in 1978. Will anyone be able to break DiMaggio's amazing record?

Baseball is filled with records, streaks, and incredible achievements. Players strive to earn a place in baseball history, but it's easier said than done. Once a player gets close to breaking a record, the spotlight shines brightly on him. It's part of what makes baseball such a fun sport to watch. With so many stats, streaks, and records in the game, players will be vying for the top spots on the charts for years to come.

# CHAPTER 1

# HITTING

▼ **Mark McGwire**

It's fun to watch a player break any record, but the home run chase is one of the most closely followed records in baseball. In 1961 Roger Maris smashed 61 home runs, passing Babe Ruth's single-season record of 60 set in 1927. Maris' record stood for 38 years.

In 1998 Sammy Sosa and Mark McGwire were on pace to break the record. Although both players surpassed Maris, McGwire was first and ended the season with 70 home runs. Sosa had 66. Only three years later, Barry Bonds notched 73 bombs, a record that still stands.

The 1998 home run chase was an exciting part of MLB history. But it's not just the power hitters who make the record books. Baseball legends Ty Cobb, Pete Rose, and Rickey Henderson weren't known for their power. Instead, they used their hitting ability and speed to enter the record books.

## HOME RUNS

▼ Hank Aaron

### CAREER ||||||||||||||||||||||||||||||||||||||||||||||

| | | | | |
|---|---|---|---|---|
| 1. | Barry Bonds | 762 | Pirates/Giants | 1986–2007 |
| 2. | Hank Aaron | 755 | Braves/Brewers | 1954–1976 |
| 3. | Babe Ruth | 714 | Red Sox/Yankees/Braves | 1914–1935 |
| 4. | Willie Mays | 660 | Giants/Mets | 1951–1952, 1954–1973 |
| 5. | Ken Griffey Jr. | 630 | Mariners/Reds/White Sox | 1989–2010 |
| 6. | Alex Rodriguez | 629 | Mariners/Rangers/Yankees | 1994–2011* |
| 7. | Sammy Sosa | 609 | Rangers/White Sox/Cubs/Orioles | 1989–2005, 2007 |
| 8. | Jim Thome | 604 | Indians/Phillies/White Sox/Dodgers/Twins | 1991–2011* |
| 9. | Frank Robinson | 586 | Reds/Orioles/Dodgers/Angels/Indians | 1956–1976 |
| 10. | Mark McGwire | 583 | Athletics/Cardinals | 1986–2001 |

*Active player

### SINGLE SEASON ||||||||||||||||||||||||||||||||||||||||||

| | | | | |
|---|---|---|---|---|
| 1. | Barry Bonds | 73 | Giants | 2001 |
| 2. | Mark McGwire | 70 | Cardinals | 1998 |
| 3. | Sammy Sosa | 66 | Cubs | 1998 |
| 4. | Mark McGwire | 65 | Cardinals | 1999 |
| 5. | Sammy Sosa | 64 | Cubs | 2001 |
| 6. | Sammy Sosa | 63 | Cubs | 1999 |
| 7. | Roger Maris | 61 | Yankees | 1961 |
| 8. | Babe Ruth | 60 | Yankees | 1927 |
| 9. | Babe Ruth | 59 | Yankees | 1921 |
| 10. | Four players tied with | 58 | | |

▲ Barry Bonds

# GRAND SLAMS

## CAREER

| | | | | |
|---|---|---|---|---|
| 1. | Lou Gehrig | 23 | Yankees | 1923–1939 |
| 2. | Alex Rodriguez | 22 | Mariners/Rangers/Yankees | 1994–2011* |
| 3. | Manny Ramirez | 21 | Indians/Red Sox/Dodgers/White Sox/Rays | 1993–2011* |
| 4. | Eddie Murray | 19 | Orioles/Dodgers/Mets/Indians/Angels | 1977–1997 |
| 5. | Willie McCovey | 18 | Giants/Padres/Athletics | 1959–1980 |
| | Robin Ventura | 18 | White Sox/Mets/Yankees/Dodgers | 1989–2004 |
| 7. | Jimmie Foxx | 17 | Athletics/Red Sox/Cubs/Phillies | 1925–1945 |
| | Ted Williams | 17 | Red Sox | 1939–1960 |
| 9. | Hank Aaron | 16 | Braves/Brewers | 1954–1976 |
| | Dave Kingman | 16 | Giants/Mets/Padres/Angels/Yankees/Cubs/Athletics | 1971–1986 |
| | Carlos Lee | 16 | White Sox/Brewers/Rangers/Astros | 1999–2011* |
| | Babe Ruth | 16 | Red Sox/Yankees/Braves | 1914–1935 |

*Active player

## SINGLE SEASON

| | | | | |
|---|---|---|---|---|
| 1. | Travis Hafner | 6 | Indians | 2006 |
| | Don Mattingly | 6 | Yankees | 1987 |
| 3. | Ernie Banks | 5 | Cubs | 1955 |
| | Jim Gentile | 5 | Orioles | 1961 |
| | Albert Pujols | 5 | Cardinals | 2009 |
| | Richie Sexson | 5 | Mariners | 2006 |
| 7. | Many players tied with | 4 | | |

▲ Travis Hafner

## RECORD FACT

The St. Louis Cardinals' Fernando Tatis set two eye-opening records April 23, 1999. He became the only player to hit two grand slams in the same inning.

Both home runs came off of Los Angeles Dodgers pitcher Chan Ho Park. The eight RBIs from the two bombs set a record for most RBIs in an inning.

## INSIDE-THE-PARK HOME RUNS

| CAREER | | | | |
|---|---|---|---|---|
| 1. | Jesse Burkett | 55 | Giants/Spiders/Perfectos/Cardinals/Browns/Americans | 1890–1905 |
| 2. | Sam Crawford | 51 | Reds/Tigers | 1899–1917 |
| 3. | Tommy Leach | 48 | Colonels/Pirates/Cubs/Reds | 1898–1915, 1918 |
| 4. | Ty Cobb | 46 | Tigers/Athletics | 1905–1928 |
| | Honus Wagner | 46 | Colonels/Pirates | 1897–1917 |
| 6. | Jake Beckley | 38 | Alleghenys/Burghers/Pirates/Giants/Reds/Cardinals | 1893–1907 |
| | Tris Speaker | 38 | Americans/Red Sox/Indians/Senators/Athletics | 1907–1928 |
| 8. | Rogers Hornsby | 33 | Cardinals/Giants/Braves/Cubs/Browns | 1915–1937 |
| 9. | Edd Roush | 31 | White Sox/Hoosiers/Pepper/Giants/Reds | 1913–1929, 1931 |
| 10. | Jake Daubert | 30 | Superbas/Dodgers/Robins/Reds | 1910–1924 |
| | Willie Keeler | 30 | Giants/Grooms/Orioles/Superbas/Highlanders | 1892–1910 |

▲ Sam Crawford

## RECORD FACT

In 1897 Tom McCreery of the Louisville Colonels slammed three in-the-park home runs in a single game.

## RUNS BATTED IN

▼ Cap Anson

### CAREER

| # | Player | RBI | Teams | Years |
|---|--------|-----|-------|-------|
| 1. | Hank Aaron | 2,297 | Braves/Brewers | 1954–1976 |
| 2. | Babe Ruth | 2,213 | Red Sox/Yankees/Braves | 1914–1935 |
| 3. | Cap Anson | 2,075 | Forest Citys/Athletics/White Stockings/Colts | 1871–1897 |
| 4. | Barry Bonds | 1,996 | Pirates/Giants | 1986–2007 |
| 5. | Lou Gehrig | 1,995 | Yankees | 1923–1939 |
| 6. | Stan Musial | 1,951 | Cardinals | 1941–1944, 1946–1963 |
| 7. | Ty Cobb | 1,938 | Tigers/Athletics | 1905–1928 |
| 8. | Jimmie Foxx | 1,922 | Athletics/Red Sox/Cubs/Phillies | 1925–1945 |
| 9. | Eddie Murray | 1,917 | Orioles/Dodgers/Mets/Indians/Angels | 1977–1997 |
| 10. | Willie Mays | 1,903 | Giants/Mets | 1951–1952, 1954–1973 |

### SINGLE SEASON

| # | Player | RBI | Team | Year |
|---|--------|-----|------|------|
| 1. | Hack Wilson | 191 | Cubs | 1930 |
| 2. | Lou Gehrig | 184 | Yankees | 1931 |
| 3. | Hank Greenberg | 183 | Tigers | 1937 |
| 4. | Jimmie Foxx | 175 | Red Sox | 1938 |
| | Lou Gehrig | 175 | Yankees | 1927 |
| 6. | Lou Gehrig | 174 | Yankees | 1930 |
| 7. | Babe Ruth | 171 | Yankees | 1921 |
| 8. | Hank Greenberg | 170 | Tigers | 1935 |
| | Chuck Klein | 170 | Phillies | 1930 |
| 10. | Jimmie Foxx | 169 | Athletics | 1932 |

▲ Babe Ruth

## RUNS BATTED IN

### SINGLE GAME |||||||||||||||||||||||||||||||||||||||||||

| 1. | Jim Bottomley | 12 | Cardinals | 1924 |
|----|---------------|-----|-----------|------|
| | Mark Whiten | 12 | Cardinals | 1993 |
| 3. | Wilbert Robinson | 11 | Orioles | 1892 |
| | Tony Lazzeri | 11 | Yankees | 1936 |
| | Phil Weintraub | 11 | Giants | 1944 |
| 6. | Eight players tied with | 10 | | |

## HALL OF FAMER
## JOSH GIBSON

The names of many amazing athletes will never appear in the record books. That's because they weren't allowed to play in the major leagues. Until Jackie Robinson broke baseball's color barrier in 1947, African-Americans played only in the Negro Leagues. Detailed records don't exist to prove it, but hard-hitting catcher Josh Gibson would most likely top many lists. Called the "black Babe Ruth," it is believed that he led the Negro National League in home runs 10 years in a row. Although his career home run total is uncertain, the Baseball Hall of Fame credits him with "almost 800 home runs."

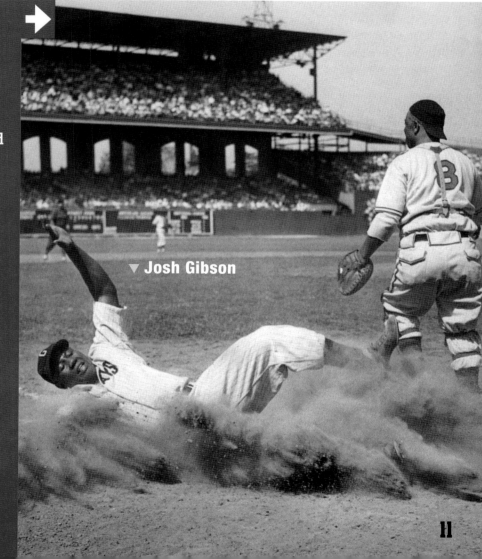

▼ Josh Gibson

▼ **Ty Cobb**

## CAREER

| | | | | |
|---|---|---|---|---|
| 1. | Rickey Henderson | 2,295 | Athletics/Yankees/ Blue Jays/Padres/ Angels/Mets/ Mariners/Red Sox/ Dodgers | 1979–2003 |
| 2. | Ty Cobb | 2,246 | Tigers/Athletics | 1905–1928 |
| 3. | Barry Bonds | 2,227 | Pirates/Giants | 1986–2007 |
| 4. | Hank Aaron | 2,174 | Braves/Brewers | 1954–1976 |
| | Babe Ruth | 2,174 | Red Sox/Yankees/ Braves | 1914–1935 |
| 6. | Pete Rose | 2,165 | Reds/Phillies/Expos | 1963–1986 |
| 7. | Willie Mays | 2,062 | Giants/Mets | 1951–1952, 1954–1973 |
| 8. | Cap Anson | 1,999 | Forest Citys/ Athletics/White Stockings/Colts | 1871–1897 |
| 9. | Stan Musial | 1,949 | Cardinals | 1941–1944, 1946–1963 |
| 10. | Lou Gehrig | 1,888 | Yankees | 1923–1939 |

**RECORD FACT**

It's hard to get on base six times in one game. But it's even harder to score six times! Only 15 players have scored six runs in a single game. Mel Ott of the New York Giants is the only player to score six times in a game twice in his career.

## SINGLE SEASON

| | | | | |
|---|---|---|---|---|
| 1. | Billy Hamilton | 198 | Phillies | 1894 |
| 2. | Tom Brown | 177 | Reds | 1891 |
| | Babe Ruth | 177 | Yankees | 1921 |
| 4. | Lou Gehrig | 167 | Yankees | 1936 |
| | Tip O'Neill | 167 | Browns | 1887 |
| 6. | Billy Hamilton | 166 | Phillies | 1895 |
| 7. | Willie Keeler | 165 | Orioles | 1894 |
| | Joe Kelley | 165 | Orioles | 1894 |
| 9. | Lou Gehrig | 163 | Yankees | 1931 |
| | Arlie Latham | 163 | Browns | 1887 |
| | Babe Ruth | 163 | Yankees | 1928 |

▲ **Billy Hamilton**

## BATTING AVERAGE

▼ Joe Jackson

### CAREER

| | | | | |
|---|---|---|---|---|
| 1. | Ty Cobb | .366 | Tigers/Athletics | 1905–1928 |
| 2. | Rogers Hornsby | .359 | Cardinals/Giants/Braves/Cubs/Browns | 1915–1937 |
| 3. | Joe Jackson | .356 | Athletics/Naps/Indians/White Sox | 1908–1920 |
| 4. | Lefty O'Doul | .349 | Yankees/Red Sox/Giants/Phillies/Robins/Dodgers | 1919–1920, 1922–1923, 1928–1934 |
| 5. | Ed Delahanty | .346 | Quakers/Infants/Phillies/Senators | 1888–1903 |
| 6. | Tris Speaker | .345 | Red Sox/Indians/Senators/Athletics | 1907–1928 |
| 7. | Billy Hamilton | .344 | Cowboys/Phillies/Beaneaters | 1888–1901 |
| | Ted Williams | .344 | Red Sox | 1939–1960 |
| 9. | Dan Brouthers | .342 | Trojans/Bisons/Wolverines/Beaneaters/Reds/Grooms/Orioles/Colonels/Phillies/Giants | 1879–1904 |
| | Babe Ruth | .342 | Red Sox/Yankees/Braves | 1914–1935 |

### SINGLE SEASON

| | | | | |
|---|---|---|---|---|
| 1. | Hugh Duffy | .440 | Beaneaters | 1894 |
| 2. | Tip O'Neill | .435 | Browns | 1887 |
| 3. | Ross Barnes | .429 | White Stockings | 1876 |
| 4. | Nap Lajoie | .427 | Athletics | 1901 |
| 5. | Willie Keeler | .424 | Orioles | 1897 |
| | Rogers Hornsby | .424 | Cardinals | 1924 |
| 7. | George Sisler | .420 | Browns | 1922 |
| | Ty Cobb | .420 | Tigers | 1911 |
| 9. | Tuck Turner | .418 | Phillies | 1894 |
| 10. | Sam Thompson | .415 | Phillies | 1894 |

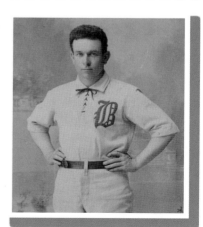

▲ Hugh Duffy

#  HITS

▼ Pete Rose

## CAREER

| | | | | |
|---|---|---|---|---|
| 1. | Pete Rose | 4,256 | Reds/Phillies/Expos | 1963–1986 |
| 2. | Ty Cobb | 4,189 | Tigers/Athletics | 1905–1928 |
| 3. | Hank Aaron | 3,771 | Braves/Brewers | 1954–1976 |
| 4. | Stan Musial | 3,630 | Cardinals | 1941–1944, 1946–1963 |
| 5. | Tris Speaker | 3,514 | Red Sox/Indians/Senators/Athletics | 1907–1928 |
| 6. | Cap Anson | 3,435 | Forest Citys/Athletics/White Stockings/Colts | 1871–1897 |
| 7. | Honus Wagner | 3,420 | Colonels/Pirates | 1897–1917 |
| 8. | Carl Yastrzemski | 3,419 | Red Sox | 1961–1983 |
| 9. | Paul Molitor | 3,319 | Brewers/Blue Jays/Twins | 1978–1998 |
| 10. | Eddie Collins | 3,315 | Athletics/White Sox | 1906–1930 |

## SINGLE SEASON

| | | | | |
|---|---|---|---|---|
| 1. | Ichiro Suzuki | 262 | Mariners | 2004 |
| 2. | George Sisler | 257 | Browns | 1920 |
| 3. | Lefty O'Doul | 254 | Phillies | 1929 |
| | Bill Terry | 254 | Giants | 1930 |
| 5. | Al Simmons | 253 | Athletics | 1925 |
| 6. | Rogers Hornsby | 250 | Cardinals | 1922 |
| | Chuck Klein | 250 | Phillies | 1930 |
| 8. | Ty Cobb | 248 | Tigers | 1911 |
| 9. | George Sisler | 246 | Browns | 1922 |
| 10. | Ichiro Suzuki | 242 | Mariners | 2001 |

▲ George Sisler

Johnny Burnett of the Cleveland Indians holds the record for most hits in a single game. He pounded out nine hits during a 1932 game, but the game lasted 18 innings. Two players have collected seven hits during a nine-inning game: Wilbert Robinson of the Baltimore Orioles and Rennie Stennett of the Pittsburgh Pirates.

## WALK AWAY FROM THE WALKS

In 1887 MLB ruled that a player's walks counted toward his hits total. But today those stats don't count on the records lists. For example, Pete Browning and Tip O'Neill each had 275 hits in 1887, which would put them at the top of the single-season hits list. But because walks counted toward their hits total that year, they don't qualify for the top 10. Ichiro Suzuki officially claims the top honor for single-season hits with 262.

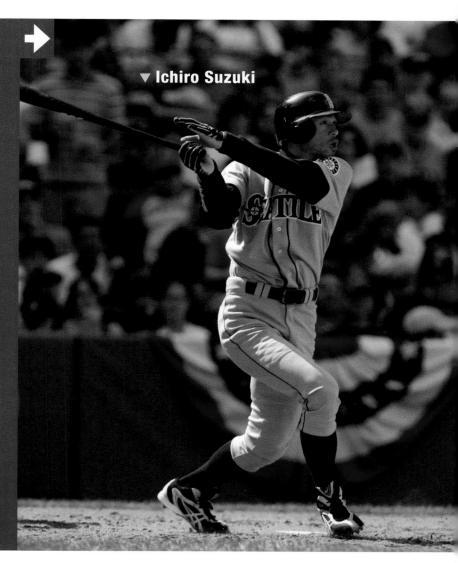

▼ Ichiro Suzuki

**SINGLES**

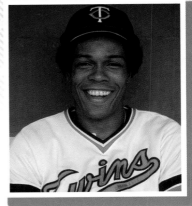
▼ **Rod Carew**

## CAREER

| # | | | | |
|---|---|---|---|---|
| 1. | Pete Rose | 3,215 | Reds/Phillies/Expos | 1963–1986 |
| 2. | Ty Cobb | 3,053 | Tigers/Athletics | 1905–1928 |
| 3. | Eddie Collins | 2,643 | Athletics/White Sox | 1906–1930 |
| 4. | Cap Anson | 2,614 | Forest Citys/Athletics/White Stockings/Colts | 1871–1897 |
| 5. | Willie Keeler | 2,513 | Giants/Grooms/Orioles/Superbas/Highlanders | 1892–1910 |
| 6. | Honus Wagner | 2,424 | Colonels/Pirates | 1897–1917 |
| 7. | Rod Carew | 2,404 | Twins/Angels | 1967–1985 |
| 8. | Tris Speaker | 2,383 | Red Sox/Indians/Senators/Athletics | 1907–1928 |
| 9. | Tony Gwynn | 2,378 | Padres | 1982–2001 |
| 10. | Paul Molitor | 2,366 | Brewers/Blue Jays/Twins | 1978–1998 |

## SINGLE SEASON

| # | | | | |
|---|---|---|---|---|
| 1. | Ichiro Suzuki | 225 | Mariners | 2004 |
| 2. | Willie Keeler | 206 | Orioles | 1898 |
| 3. | Ichiro Suzuki | 203 | Mariners | 2007 |
| 4. | Lloyd Waner | 198 | Pirates | 1927 |
| 5. | Willie Keeler | 193 | Orioles | 1897 |
| 6. | Ichiro Suzuki | 192 | Mariners | 2001 |
| 7. | Jesse Burkett | 191 | Spiders | 1896 |
| 8. | Willie Keeler | 190 | Superbas | 1899 |
| 9. | Wade Boggs | 187 | Red Sox | 1985 |
| 10. | Jesse Burkett | 186 | Spiders | 1898 |
| | Ichiro Suzuki | 186 | Mariners | 2006 |

▲ **Ichiro Suzuki**

 # DOUBLES

## CAREER

| | | | | |
|---|---|---|---|---|
| 1. | Tris Speaker | 792 | Red Sox/Indians/Senators/Athletics | 1907–1928 |
| 2. | Pete Rose | 746 | Reds/Phillies/Expos | 1963–1986 |
| 3. | Stan Musial | 725 | Cardinals | 1941–1944, 1946–1963 |
| 4. | Ty Cobb | 724 | Tigers/Athletics | 1905–1928 |
| 5. | Craig Biggio | 668 | Astros | 1988–2007 |
| 6. | George Brett | 665 | Royals | 1973–1993 |
| 7. | Nap Lajoie | 657 | Phillies/Athletics/Bronchos/Naps | 1896–1916 |
| 8. | Carl Yastrzemski | 646 | Red Sox | 1961–1983 |
| 9. | Honus Wagner | 643 | Colonels/Pirates | 1897–1917 |
| 10. | Hank Aaron | 624 | Braves/Brewers | 1954–1976 |

## SINGLE SEASON

| | | | | |
|---|---|---|---|---|
| 1. | Earl Webb | 67 | Red Sox | 1931 |
| 2. | George Burns | 64 | Indians | 1926 |
| | Joe Medwick | 64 | Cardinals | 1936 |
| 4. | Hank Greenberg | 63 | Tigers | 1934 |
| 5. | Paul Waner | 62 | Pirates | 1932 |
| 6. | Charlie Gehringer | 60 | Tigers | 1936 |
| 7. | Todd Helton | 59 | Rockies | 2000 |
| | Chuck Klein | 59 | Phillies | 1930 |
| | Tris Speaker | 59 | Indians | 1923 |
| 10. | Carlos Delgado | 57 | Blue Jays | 2000 |
| | Billy Herman | 57 | Cubs | 1935 |
| | Billy Herman | 57 | Cubs | 1936 |

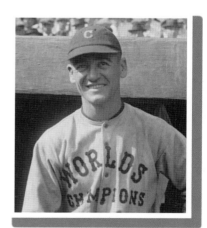

▲ George Burns

# TRIPLES

## CAREER

| | | | | |
|---|---|---|---|---|
| 1. | Sam Crawford | 309 | Reds/Tigers | 1899–1917 |
| 2. | Ty Cobb | 295 | Tigers/Athletics | 1905–1928 |
| 3. | Honus Wagner | 252 | Colonels/Pirates | 1897–1917 |
| 4. | Jake Beckley | 244 | Alleghenys/Burghers/Pirates/Giants/Reds/Cardinals | 1893–1907 |
| 5. | Roger Connor | 233 | Trojans/Gothams/Giants/Phillies/Browns | 1880–1897 |
| 6. | Tris Speaker | 222 | Red Sox/Indians/Senators/Athletics | 1907–1928 |
| 7. | Fred Clarke | 220 | Colonels/Pirates | 1894–1911, 1913–1915 |
| 8. | Dan Brouthers | 205 | Trojans/Bisons/Wolverines/Beaneaters/Reds/Grooms/Orioles/Colonels/Phillies/Giants | 1879–1904 |
| 9. | Joe Kelley | 198 | Beaneaters/Pirates/Orioles/Superbas/Reds/Doves | 1891–1906 |
| 10. | Paul Waner | 191 | Pirates/Dodgers/Braves/Yankees | 1926–1945 |

## SINGLE SEASON

| | | | | |
|---|---|---|---|---|
| 1. | Chief Wilson | 36 | Pirates | 1912 |
| 2. | Dave Orr | 31 | Metropolitans | 1886 |
| | Heinie Reitz | 31 | Orioles | 1894 |
| 4. | Perry Werden | 29 | Browns | 1893 |
| 5. | Harry Davis | 28 | Pirates | 1897 |
| | Sam Thompson | 28 | Phillies | 1894 |
| 7. | George Davis | 27 | Giants | 1893 |
| 8. | Five players tied with | 26 | | |

▲ Harry Davis

# STOLEN BASES

## CAREER

| | | | | |
|---|---|---|---|---|
| 1. | Rickey Henderson | 1,406 | Athletics/Yankees/Blue Jays/Padres/Angels/Mets/Mariners/Red Sox/Dodgers | 1979–2003 |
| 2. | Lou Brock | 938 | Cubs/Cardinals | 1961–1979 |
| 3. | Billy Hamilton | 914 | Cowboys/Phillies/Beaneaters | 1888–1901 |
| 4. | Ty Cobb | 897 | Tigers/Athletics | 1905–1928 |
| 5. | Tim Raines | 808 | Expos/White Sox/Yankees/Athletics/Orioles/Marlins | 1979–1999, 2001–2002 |
| 6. | Vince Coleman | 752 | Cardinals/Mets/Royals/Mariners/Reds/Tigers | 1985–1997 |
| 7. | Arlie Latham | 742 | Bisons/Browns/Pirates/Reds/Senators/Giants | 1880, 1883–1896, 1899, 1909 |
| 8. | Eddie Collins | 741 | Athletics/White Sox | 1906–1930 |
| 9. | Max Carey | 738 | Pirates/Robins | 1910–1929 |
| 10. | Honus Wagner | 723 | Colonels/Pirates | 1897–1917 |

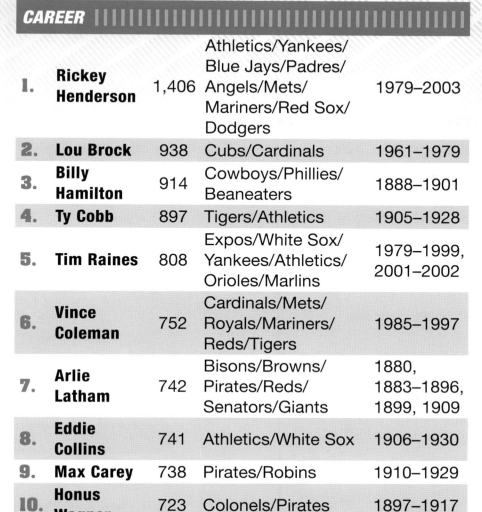

## SINGLE SEASON

| | | | | |
|---|---|---|---|---|
| 1. | Hugh Nicol | 138 | Red Stockings | 1887 |
| 2. | Rickey Henderson | 130 | Athletics | 1982 |
| 3. | Arlie Latham | 129 | Browns | 1887 |
| 4. | Lou Brock | 118 | Cardinals | 1974 |
| 5. | Charlie Comiskey | 117 | Browns | 1887 |
| 6. | Billy Hamilton | 111 | Cowboys | 1889 |
| | Billy Hamilton | 111 | Phillies | 1891 |
| | Monte Ward | 111 | Giants | 1887 |
| 9. | Vince Coleman | 110 | Cardinals | 1985 |
| 10. | Vince Coleman | 109 | Cardinals | 1987 |

▲ Lou Brock

## ⚾ WALKS

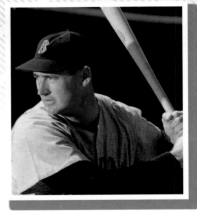

### CAREER ||||||||||||||||||||||||||||||||||||||||||||||||||||||

| | | | | |
|---|---|---|---|---|
| 1. | Barry Bonds | 2,558 | Pirates/Giants | 1986–2007 |
| 2. | Rickey Henderson | 2,190 | Athletics/Yankees/ Blue Jays/Padres/ Angels/Mets/ Mariners/Red Sox/ Dodgers | 1979–2003 |
| 3. | Babe Ruth | 2,062 | Red Sox/Yankees/ Braves | 1914–1935 |
| 4. | Ted Williams | 2,021 | Red Sox | 1939–1960 |
| 5. | Joe Morgan | 1,865 | Colt .45s/Astros/ Reds/Giants/ Phillies/Athletics | 1963–1984 |
| 6. | Carl Yastrzemski | 1,845 | Red Sox | 1961–1983 |
| 7. | Mickey Mantle | 1,733 | Yankees | 1951–1968 |
| 8. | Jim Thome | 1,725 | Indians/Phillies/ White Sox/ Dodgers/Twins | 1991–2011* |
| 9. | Mel Ott | 1,708 | Giants | 1926–1947 |
| 10. | Frank Thomas | 1,667 | White Sox/ Athletics/Blue Jays | 1990–2008 |

*Active player

### SINGLE SEASON ||||||||||||||||||||||||||||||||||||||||||||||

| | | | | |
|---|---|---|---|---|
| 1. | Barry Bonds | 232 | Giants | 2004 |
| 2. | Barry Bonds | 198 | Giants | 2002 |
| 3. | Barry Bonds | 177 | Giants | 2005 |
| 4. | Babe Ruth | 170 | Yankees | 1923 |
| 5. | Mark McGwire | 162 | Cardinals | 1998 |
| | Ted Williams | 162 | Red Sox | 1947 |
| | Ted Williams | 162 | Red Sox | 1949 |
| 8. | Ted Williams | 156 | Red Sox | 1946 |
| 9. | Barry Bonds | 151 | Giants | 1996 |
| | Eddie Yost | 151 | Senators | 1956 |

### RECORD FACT

When it comes to intentional walks, Barry Bonds is the king. Pitchers often avoided the slugger's mighty swing by giving him a free ride to first base. Bonds tops the list with 688 career intentional walks. Hank Aaron comes in second with 293—less than half of Bonds' total. In 2004 Bonds was intentionally walked 120 times, which was about one in five plate appearances.

# HIT BY PITCH

**CAREER** |||||||||||||||||||||||||||||||||||||||||||||||||||

| | | | | |
|---|---|---|---|---|
| 1. | Hughie Jennings | 287 | Colonels/Orioles/Superbas/Phillies/Tigers | 1891–1903, 1907, 1909–1910, 1912, 1918 |
| 2. | Craig Biggio | 285 | Astros | 1988–2007 |
| 3. | Tommy Tucker | 272 | Orioles/Beaneaters/Senators/Bridegrooms/Browns/Spiders | 1887–1899 |
| 4. | Don Baylor | 267 | Orioles/Athletics/Angels/Yankees/Red Sox/Twins | 1970–1988 |
| 5. | Jason Kendall | 254 | Pirates/Athletics/Cubs/Brewers/Royals | 1996–2010 |
| 6. | Ron Hunt | 243 | Mets/Dodgers/Giants/Expos/Cardinals | 1963–1974 |
| 7. | Dan McGann | 230 | Beaneaters/Orioles/Superbas/Senators/Cardinals/Giants/Doves | 1896, 1898–1908 |
| 8. | Frank Robinson | 198 | Redlegs/Reds/Orioles/Dodgers/Angels/Indians | 1956–1976 |
| 9. | Minnie Minoso | 192 | Indians/White Sox/Cardinals/Senators | 1949, 1951–1964, 1976, 1980 |
| 10. | Jake Beckley | 183 | Alleghenys/Burghers/Pirates/Giants/Reds/Cardinals | 1888–1907 |

**RECORD FACT** Only two players have been hit by a pitch 50 or more times in one season. Hughie Jennings of the Baltimore Orioles was plunked 51 times in 1896. Seventy-five years later, the Montreal Expos' Ron Hunt was hit by 50 pitches. It must have been an unlucky season for Hunt—his next highest single-season total was 26.

# CHAPTER 2

# PITCHING

▼ Orel Hershiser

The Los Angeles Dodgers were firmly atop the NL West in September 1988. Their ace, Orel Hershiser, took the mound September 5 to face the Atlanta Braves. Nine dominant innings later, Hershiser had shut out the Braves for the complete game. Notch another win on his belt, and the Dodgers were one step closer to the playoffs.

Hershiser took the mound again September 10, and he pulled off another shutout, this time against the Cincinnati Reds. He followed up the performance with shutouts against the Atlanta Braves, Houston Astros, and San Francisco Giants. By the time he stepped onto the mound against the San Diego Padres September 28, he had pitched 49 consecutive scoreless innings. (He started the streak August 30 when he pitched four scoreless innings against the Montreal Expos.)

All eyes were on Hershiser as he continued to put zeroes on the scoreboard. Each scoreless inning brought him closer to Don Drysdale's streak of 58.2 innings. By the end of the ninth inning, Hershiser's streak reached 58 innings. But the game wasn't over. Tied 0-0, it went into extra innings, and Hershiser stayed in the game. He completed the 10th inning without giving up a run, and the record was his—59 consecutive scoreless innings.

## CAREER

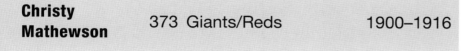

| | | | | |
|---|---|---|---|---|
| 1. | Cy Young | 511 | Spiders/Perfectos/Cardinals/Americans/Naps/Rustlers | 1890–1911 |
| 2. | Walter Johnson | 417 | Senators | 1907–1927 |
| 3. | Grover Alexander | 373 | Phillies/Cubs/Cardinals | 1911–1930 |
| | Christy Mathewson | 373 | Giants/Reds | 1900–1916 |
| 5. | Pud Galvin | 365 | Brown Stockings/Bisons/Alleghenys/Burghers/Pirates/Browns | 1875, 1879–1892 |
| 6. | Warren Spahn | 363 | Braves/Mets/Giants | 1942, 1946–1965 |
| 7. | Kid Nichols | 361 | Beaneaters/Cardinals/Phillies | 1890–1901, 1904–1906 |
| 8. | Greg Maddux | 355 | Cubs/Braves/Dodgers/Padres | 1986–2008 |
| 9. | Roger Clemens | 354 | Red Sox/Blue Jays/Yankees/Astros | 1984–2007 |
| 10. | Tim Keefe | 342 | Trojans/Metropolitans/Giants/Phillies | 1880–1993 |

## SINGLE SEASON

| | | | | |
|---|---|---|---|---|
| 1. | Charles Radbourn | 59 | Grays | 1884 |
| 2. | John Clarkson | 53 | White Stockings | 1885 |
| 3. | Guy Hecker | 52 | Eclipse | 1884 |
| 4. | John Clarkson | 49 | Beaneaters | 1889 |
| 5. | Charlie Buffinton | 48 | Beaneaters | 1884 |
| | Charles Radbourn | 48 | Grays | 1883 |
| 7. | Al Spalding | 47 | White Stockings | 1876 |
| | Monte Ward | 47 | Grays | 1879 |
| 9. | Pud Galvin | 46 | Bisons | 1883 |
| | Pud Galvin | 46 | Bisons | 1884 |
| | Matt Kilroy | 46 | Orioles | 1887 |

▲ John Clarkson

# STRIKEOUTS

| | | | | |
|---|---|---|---|---|
| 1. | Nolan Ryan | 5,714 | Mets/Angels/Astros/Rangers | 1966, 1968–1993 |
| 2. | Randy Johnson | 4,875 | Expos/Mariners/Astros/Diamondbacks/Yankees/Giants | 1988–2009 |
| 3. | Roger Clemens | 4,672 | Red Sox/Blue Jays/Yankees/Astros | 1984–2007 |
| 4. | Steve Carlton | 4,136 | Cardinals/Phillies/Giants/White Sox/Indians/Twins | 1965–1988 |
| 5. | Bert Blyleven | 3,701 | Twins/Rangers/Pirates/Indians/Angels | 1970–1990, 1992 |
| 6. | Tom Seaver | 3,640 | Mets/Reds/White Sox/Red Sox | 1967–1986 |
| 7. | Don Sutton | 3,574 | Dodgers/Astros/Brewers/Athletics/Angels | 1966–1988 |
| 8. | Gaylord Perry | 3,534 | Giants/Indians/Rangers/Padres/Yankees/Braves/Mariners/Royals | 1962–1983 |
| 9. | Walter Johnson | 3,509 | Senators | 1907–1927 |
| 10. | Greg Maddux | 3,371 | Cubs/Braves/Dodgers/Padres | 1986–2008 |

| | | | | |
|---|---|---|---|---|
| 1. | Matt Kilroy | 513 | Orioles | 1886 |
| 2. | Toad Ramsey | 499 | Colonels | 1886 |
| 3. | Hugh Daily | 483 | Chicago/Pittsburgh/Nationals | 1884 |
| 4. | Dupee Shaw | 451 | Wolverines/Reds | 1884 |
| 5. | Charles Radbourn | 441 | Grays | 1884 |
| 6. | Charlie Buffinton | 417 | Beaneaters | 1884 |
| 7. | Guy Hecker | 385 | Eclipse | 1884 |
| 8. | Nolan Ryan | 383 | Angels | 1973 |
| 9. | Sandy Koufax | 382 | Dodgers | 1965 |
| 10. | Bill Sweeney | 374 | Monumentals | 1884 |

▲ Sandy Koufax

# INNINGS PITCHED

## CAREER

| # | Player | IP | Teams | Years |
|---|--------|-----|-------|-------|
| 1. | Cy Young | 7,356 | Spiders/Perfectos/Cardinals/Americans/Naps/Rustlers | 1890–1911 |
| 2. | Pud Galvin | 6,003.1 | Brown Stockings/Bisons/Alleghenys/Burghers/Pirates/Browns | 1875, 1879–1892 |
| 3. | Walter Johnson | 5,914.1 | Senators | 1907–1927 |
| 4. | Phil Niekro | 5,404 | Braves/Yankees/Indians/Blue Jays | 1964–1987 |
| 5. | Nolan Ryan | 5,386 | Mets/Angels/Astros/Rangers | 1966, 1968–1993 |
| 6. | Gaylord Perry | 5,350 | Giants/Indians/Rangers/Padres/Yankees/Mariners/Royals | 1962–1983 |
| 7. | Don Sutton | 5,282.1 | Dodgers/Astros/Brewers/Athletics/Angels | 1966–1988 |
| 8. | Warren Spahn | 5,243.2 | Braves/Mets/Giants | 1942, 1946–1965 |
| 9. | Steve Carlton | 5,217.2 | Cardinals/Phillies/Giants/White Sox/Indians/Twins | 1965–1988 |
| 10. | Grover Alexander | 5,190 | Phillies/Cubs/Cardinals | 1911–1930 |

## SINGLE SEASON

| # | Player | IP | Team | Year |
|---|--------|-----|------|------|
| 1. | Will White | 680.0 | Reds | 1879 |
| 2. | Charles Radbourn | 678.2 | Grays | 1884 |
| 3. | Guy Hecker | 670.2 | Eclipse | 1884 |
| 4. | Jim McCormick | 657.2 | Blues | 1880 |
| 5. | Pud Galvin | 656.1 | Bisons | 1883 |
| 6. | Pud Galvin | 636.1 | Bisons | 1884 |
| 7. | Charles Radbourn | 632.1 | Grays | 1883 |
| 8. | John Clarkson | 623.0 | White Stockings | 1885 |
| 9. | Jim Devlin | 622.0 | Grays | 1876 |
|  | Bill Hutchinson | 622.0 | Colts | 1892 |

▲ Jim McCormick

# EARNED RUN AVERAGE (ERA)

## CAREER

| | | | | |
|---|---|---|---|---|
| 1. | Ed Walsh | 1.82 | White Sox/Braves | 1904–1917 |
| 2. | Addie Joss | 1.89 | Bronchos/Naps | 1902–1910 |
| 3. | Jim Devlin | 1.90 | White Stockings/Grays | 1875–1877 |
| 4. | Jack Pfiester | 2.02 | Pirates/Cubs | 1903–1904, 1906–1911 |
| 5. | Joe Wood | 2.03 | Red Sox/Indians | 1908–1915, 1917, 1919–1920 |
| 6. | Mordecai Brown | 2.06 | Cardinals/Cubs/Reds/Terriers/Tip-Tops/Whales | 1903–1916 |
| 7. | Monte Ward | 2.10 | Grays/Gothams | 1878–1884 |
| 8. | Christy Mathewson | 2.13 | Giants/Reds | 1900–1916 |
| | Al Spalding | 2.13 | Red Stockings/White Stockings | 1871–1877 |
| 10. | Tommy Bond | 2.14 | Atlantics/Dark Blues/Red Stockings/Ruby Legs/Reds/Hoosiers | 1874–1882, 1884 |

## SINGLE SEASON

| | | | | |
|---|---|---|---|---|
| 1. | Tim Keefe | 0.86 | Trojans | 1880 |
| 2. | Dutch Leonard | 0.96 | Red Sox | 1914 |
| 3. | Mordecai Brown | 1.04 | Cubs | 1906 |
| 4. | Bob Gibson | 1.12 | Cardinals | 1968 |
| 5. | Christy Mathewson | 1.14 | Giants | 1909 |
| | Walter Johnson | 1.14 | Senators | 1913 |
| 7. | Jack Pfiester | 1.15 | Cubs | 1907 |
| 8. | Addie Joss | 1.16 | Naps | 1908 |
| 9. | Carl Lundgren | 1.17 | Cubs | 1907 |
| 10. | Denny Driscoll | 1.21 | Alleghenys | 1882 |

▲ Tim Keefe

## PERFECT PITCHERS

Any pitcher would be happy to go nine innings without allowing a run for a shutout. To not give up any hits over those nine innings would be even more impressive. But to throw a perfect game—not allowing any hits, walks, errors, or hit batters—is a rare accomplishment. Only 21 players have thrown perfect games in the majors. The youngest pitcher to pull off a perfect game was 20-year-old John Ward for the Providence Grays in 1880. The oldest was Randy Johnson, who completed a perfect game for the Arizona Diamondbacks in 2004 at age 40.

▼ Randy Johnson

**RECORD FACT** Chicago White Sox pitcher Mark Buehrle set a pitching record in 2009. He retired 45 batters in a row, breaking the previous record of 41.

# SHUTOUTS

▼ **Walter Johnson**

## CAREER ||||||||||||||||||||||||||||||||||||||||||||||||

| | | | | |
|---|---|---|---|---|
| 1. | Walter Johnson | 110 | Senators | 1907–1927 |
| 2. | Grover Alexander | 90 | Phillies/Cubs/ Cardinals | 1911–1930 |
| 3. | Christy Mathewson | 79 | Giants/Reds | 1900–1916 |
| 4. | Cy Young | 76 | Spiders/Perfectos/ Cardinals/Americans/ Naps/Rustlers | 1890–1911 |
| 5. | Eddie Plank | 69 | Athletics/Terriers/ Browns | 1901–1917 |
| 6. | Warren Spahn | 63 | Braves/Mets/Giants | 1942, 1946–1965 |
| 7. | Nolan Ryan | 61 | Mets/Angels/Astros/ Rangers | 1966, 1968–1993 |
| | Tom Seaver | 61 | Mets/Reds/White Sox/Red Sox | 1967–1986 |
| 9. | Bert Blyleven | 60 | Twins/Rangers/ Pirates/Indians/Angels | 1970–1990, 1992 |
| 10. | Don Sutton | 58 | Dodgers/Astros/ Brewers/Athletics/ Angels | 1966–1988 |

## SINGLE SEASON |||||||||||||||||||||||||||||||||||||||

| | | | | |
|---|---|---|---|---|
| 1. | Grover Alexander | 16 | Phillies | 1916 |
| | George Bradley | 16 | Brown Stockings | 1876 |
| 3. | Jack Coombs | 13 | Athletics | 1910 |
| | Bob Gibson | 13 | Cardinals | 1968 |
| 5. | Grover Alexander | 12 | Phillies | 1915 |
| | Pud Galvin | 12 | Bisons | 1884 |
| | Ed Morris | 12 | Alleghenys | 1886 |
| 8. | Eight players tied with | 11 | | |

▲ **Grover Alexander**

## ⚾ SHUTOUTS

### CONSECUTIVE SHUTOUT INNINGS PITCHED

| | | | | |
|---|---|---|---|---|
| 1. | Orel Hershiser | 59.0 | Dodgers | 1988 |
| 2. | Don Drysdale | 58.2 | Dodgers | 1968 |
| 3. | Walter Johnson | 55.2 | Senators | 1913 |
| 4. | Jack Coombs | 53.0 | Athletics | 1910 |
| 5. | Bob Gibson | 47.0 | Cardinals | 1968 |
| 6. | Carl Hubbell | 45.1 | Giants | 1933 |
| 7. | Cy Young | 45.0 | Americans | 1904 |
| | Doc White | 45.0 | White Sox | 1904 |
| | Sal Maglie | 45.0 | Giants | 1950 |
| 10. | Ed Reulbach | 44.0 | Cubs | 1908 |

## STRIKEOUT ACES

Only four pitchers in MLB history have struck out at least 20 batters in a single game. Tom Cheney sent 21 batters back to the dugout over 16 innings in 1962. In 1986 Roger Clemens struck out 20 batters, then repeated the feat 10 years later. In only his fifth major league game, Kerry Wood mowed down 20 hitters in a one-hit masterpiece in 1998. In 2001 Randy Johnson struck out 20 batters over nine innings, but he was replaced when the game went to extra innings.

▼ **Kerry Wood**

## RECORD FACT

Nolan Ryan is not just the strikeout king. He is also firmly atop the no-hitter records list with seven. The no-hitters occurred during an 18-year span with three teams: the California Angels, Houston Astros, and Texas Rangers.

# CY YOUNG WINNERS

Cy Young, the all-time wins leader, had an award named after him in 1956. The annual award honors the two best pitchers, one from the American League and one from the National League.

## LEADERS ||||||||||||||||||

| 1. | Roger Clemens | 7 |
|---|---|---|
| 2. | Randy Johnson | 5 |
| 3. | Steve Carlton | 4 |
| | Greg Maddux | 4 |
| 5. | Sandy Koufax | 3 |
| | Pedro Martinez | 3 |
| | Jim Palmer | 3 |
| | Tom Seaver | 3 |
| 9. | Many players tied with | 2 |

▲ Roger Clemens

**RECORD FACT** In 1985 Dwight Gooden became the youngest pitcher to win the Cy Young award. The 20-year-old hurler collected 268 strikeouts and eight shutouts that season.

## NO RELIEF NEEDED

Two players have pitched 26 innings in a single game: Leon Cadore of the Brooklyn Robins and Joe Oeschger of the Boston Braves. The pitchers squared off May 1, 1920. The Robins scored in the top of the fifth, but the Braves tied it up in the bottom of the sixth. Then Cadore and Oeschger matched each other scoreless inning after scoreless inning. After the 26th inning, the game was declared a tie. The 26-inning marathon ranks as the longest game in MLB history.

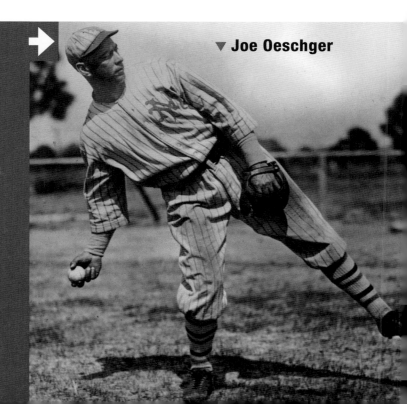

▼ Joe Oeschger

# SAVES

▼ Mariano Rivera

## CAREER ||||||||||||||||||||||||||||||||||||||||||||||

| | | | | |
|---|---|---|---|---|
| 1. | Mariano Rivera | 603 | Yankees | 1995–2011* |
| 2. | Trevor Hoffman | 601 | Marlins/Padres/ Brewers | 1993–2010 |
| 3. | Lee Smith | 478 | Cubs/Red Sox/ Cardinals/Yankees/ Orioles/Angels/Reds/ Expos | 1980–1997 |
| 4. | John Franco | 424 | Reds/Mets/Astros | 1984–2001, 2003–2005 |
| 5. | Billy Wagner | 422 | Astros/Phillies/Mets/ Red Sox/Braves | 1995–2010 |
| 6. | Dennis Eckersley | 390 | Indians/Red Sox/Cubs/ Athletics/Cardinals | 1975–1998 |
| 7. | Jeff Reardon | 367 | Mets/Expos/Twins/ Red Sox/Braves/Reds/ Yankees | 1979–1994 |
| 8. | Troy Percival | 358 | Angels/Tigers/ Cardinals/Rays | 1995–2005, 2007–2009 |
| 9. | Randy Myers | 347 | Mets/Reds/Padres/ Cubs/Orioles/Blue Jays | 1985–1998 |
| 10. | Rollie Fingers | 341 | Athletics/Padres/ Brewers | 1968–1982, 1984–1985 |

*Active player

## SINGLE SEASON |||||||||||||||||||||||||||||||||||||||

| | | | | |
|---|---|---|---|---|
| 1. | Francisco Rodriguez | 62 | Angels | 2008 |
| 2. | Bobby Thigpen | 57 | White Sox | 1990 |
| 3. | Eric Gagne | 55 | Dodgers | 2003 |
| | John Smoltz | 55 | Braves | 2002 |
| 5. | Trevor Hoffman | 53 | Padres | 1998 |
| | Randy Myers | 53 | Cubs | 1993 |
| | Mariano Rivera | 53 | Yankees | 2004 |
| 8. | Eric Gagne | 52 | Dodgers | 2002 |
| 9. | Rod Beck | 51 | Cubs | 1998 |
| | Dennis Eckersley | 51 | Athletics | 1992 |

▲ Francisco Rodriguez

# CHAPTER 3

# TEAMS

▼ Alex Rodriguez of the New York Yankees

Most teams go through the highs of winning and the lows of defeat. But every now and then a franchise goes through such an amazing period of success that it becomes known as a dynasty.

The New York Yankees have experienced several dynasties in team history. From Babe Ruth and Lou Gehrig to Derek Jeter and Alex Rodriguez, the team has boasted its fair share of baseball greats. The Yankees definitely know how to win.

It might seem strange to compare the Yankees to the Chicago Cubs— a franchise that hasn't won a World Series in more than 100 years. But many sports experts say that the 1906 Cubs were part of one of baseball's greatest teams. Although they lost the World Series that year, they bounced back to win the championship in 1907 and 1908. Their 116–36 record in 1906 still stands as the best single-season team winning percentage.

▼ Babe Ruth of the Yankees & John McGraw of the Giants

### BEST (FRANCHISE HISTORY) ||||||||||||||||||||||||||||||

| 1. | New York Yankees | 56.8% | 9,767–7,426 |
|----|------------------|-------|-------------|
| 2. | San Francisco Giants | 53.8% | 10,522–9,034 |
| 3. | Los Angeles Dodgers | 52.4% | 10,217–9,278 |
| 4. | Boston Red Sox | 51.8% | 8,909–8,305 |
| | St. Louis Cardinals | 51.8% | 10,195–9,490 |
| 6. | Chicago Cubs | 51.3% | 10,311–9,779 |
| 7. | Cleveland Indians | 50.9% | 8,771–8,449 |
| 8. | Cincinnati Reds | 50.7% | 9,994–9,702 |
| | Detroit Tigers | 50.7% | 8,740–8,504 |
| 10. | Chicago White Sox | 50.6% | 8,707–8,496 |

### BEST (SINGLE SEASON) ||||||||||||||||||||||||||||||

| 1. | Chicago Cubs | 76.3% | 1906 | 116–36 |
|----|--------------|-------|------|--------|
| 2. | Pittsburgh Pirates | 74.1% | 1902 | 103–36 |
| 3. | Chicago White Stockings | 72.6% | 1886 | 90–34 |
| 4. | Pittsburgh Pirates | 72.4% | 1909 | 110–42 |
| 5. | Cleveland Indians | 72.1% | 1954 | 111–43 |
| 6. | Seattle Mariners | 71.6% | 2001 | 116–46 |
| 7. | New York Yankees | 71.4% | 1927 | 110–44 |
| 8. | Detroit Wolverines | 70.7% | 1886 | 87–36 |
| 9. | Boston Beaneaters | 70.5% | 1897 | 93–39 |
| 10. | Chicago Cubs | 70.4% | 1907 | 107–45 |

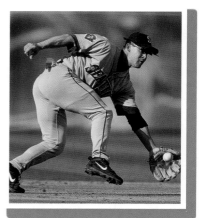

▲ Brett Boone of the Seattle Mariners

**RECORD FACT** Ties were common in baseball games in the early 1900s. Since ties are not considered wins or losses, they don't count toward a team's win-loss record.

## WIN-LOSS PERCENTAGE

▼ **Wade Boggs of the Tampa Bay Rays**

| WORST (FRANCHISE HISTORY) | | |
|---|---|---|
| 1. Tampa Bay Rays | 44.7% | 1,013–1,252 |
| 2. San Diego Padres | 46.3% | 3,169–3,671 |
| 3. Seattle Mariners | 46.7% | 2,589–2,956 |
| 4. Philadelphia Phillies | 47.3% | 9,237–10,292 |
| 5. Baltimore Orioles | 47.4% | 8,148–9,052 |
| Texas Rangers | 47.4% | 3,843–4,272 |
| 7. Washington Nationals | 47.5% | 3,247–3,583 |
| 8. Colorado Rockies | 47.6% | 1,437–1,579 |
| 9. Florida Marlins | 47.7% | 1,435–1,575 |
| Milwaukee Brewers | 47.7% | 3,262–3,571 |

| WORST (SINGLE SEASON) | | | |
|---|---|---|---|
| 1. Cleveland Spiders | 13.0% | 1899 | 20–134 |
| 2. Pittsburgh Alleghenys | 16.9% | 1890 | 23–113 |
| 3. Philadelphia Athletics | 23.5% | 1916 | 36–117 |
| 4. Boston Braves | 24.8% | 1935 | 38–115 |
| 5. New York Mets | 25.0% | 1962 | 40–120 |
| 6. Washington Senators | 25.2% | 1904 | 38–113 |
| 7. Philadelphia Athletics | 25.7% | 1919 | 36–104 |
| 8. St. Louis Browns | 26.0% | 1898 | 39–111 |
| 9. Detroit Tigers | 26.5% | 2003 | 43–119 |
| 10. Pittsburgh Pirates | 27.3% | 1952 | 42–112 |

▲ **Guy Hecker of the Pittsburgh Alleghenys**

**RECORD FACT** Between 1999 and 2001, the Cincinnati Reds went 208 straight games without being shut out.

# STREAKS

▼ Tim Hudson of the
Oakland Athletics

## WINS

| | | | |
|---|---|---|---|
| 1. | New York Giants | 26 | 1916 |
| 2. | Chicago White Stockings | 21 | 1880 |
| | Chicago Cubs | 21 | 1935 |
| 4. | Providence Grays | 20 | 1884 |
| | Oakland Athletics | 20 | 2002 |
| | St. Louis Maroons | 20 | 1884 |

## LOSSES

| | | | |
|---|---|---|---|
| 1. | Louisville Colonels | 26 | 1889 |
| 2. | Cleveland Spiders | 24 | 1899 |
| 3. | Pittsburgh Alleghenys | 23 | 1890 |
| | Philadelphia Phillies | 23 | 1961 |
| 5. | Philadelphia Athletics | 22 | 1890 |

▲ Paul Cook of the
Louisville Colonels

## A TIE ISN'T A LOSS

The New York Giants hold the record for the longest winning streak in MLB history. But their 26-game streak spanned 27 games. After winning the first 12 games, they tied the Pittsburgh Pirates. Then they won the next 14 games before losing to the Boston Braves.

▼ Benny Kauf of the
New York Giants

| | | | |
|---|---|---|---|
| **Most runs scored in an inning** | 18 | Chicago White Stockings | 1883 |
| **Most runs scored in a game** | 36 | Chicago Colts | 1897 |
| **Most runs scored in a game, both teams** | 49 | Chicago Cubs and Philadelphia Phillies | 1922 |
| **Most runs scored in a season** | 1,220 | Boston Beaneaters | 1894 |
| **Most hits in a game** | 33 | Cleveland Indians | 1932 |
| **Most hits in a season** | 1,783 | Philadelphia Phillies | 1930 |
| **Most home runs in a game** | 10 | Toronto Blue Jays | 1987 |
| **Most home runs in a season** | 264 | Seattle Mariners | 1997 |
| **Most strikeouts in a season** | 1,529 | Arizona Diamondbacks | 2010 |
| **Lowest ERA in a season** | 1.73 | Chicago Cubs | 1907 |

## SLOW START

The Baltimore Orioles had a 21-game losing streak in 1988. That's a tough stretch of games, but it doesn't make the top five for longest losing streaks. However, the first loss of the Orioles' streak came on Opening Day. Almost a full month passed before they won their first game. They hold the unflattering record for worst start to a season.

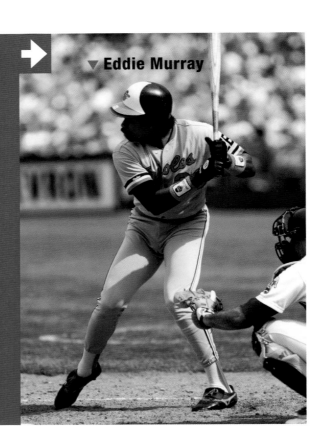

▼ Eddie Murray

**RECORD FACT** The Detroit Tigers and Chicago White Sox have combined for the most home runs in a game—twice! The two teams hammered out 12 home runs May 28, 1995, with the Tigers sending out seven. They repeated the feat July 2, 2002, with both teams pounding out six homers.

▲ **Prince Fielder of the '06 Brewers**

| | |
|---|---|
| New York Giants | June 6, 1939 |
| Philadelphia Phillies | June 2, 1949 |
| San Francisco Giants | August 23, 1961 |
| Minnesota Twins | June 9, 1966 |
| Milwaukee Brewers | April 22, 2006 |

The Minnesota Twins collected their home runs against the Kansas City Athletics. The Cincinnati Reds were on the losing end in the other four games. And that's a record in itself!

## OUT OF THE PARK

Sixteen players in MLB history have hit four home runs in a single game. Hall of Famers Lou Gehrig, Willie Mays, and Mike Schmidt each achieved the feat. For two players, Ed Delahanty and Bob Horner, four home runs were not enough to win the game. Their teams lost despite the players' heroic hitting efforts.

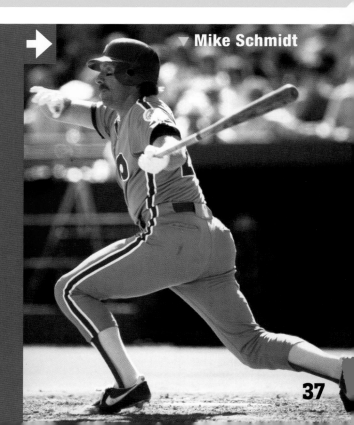

▼ Mike Schmidt

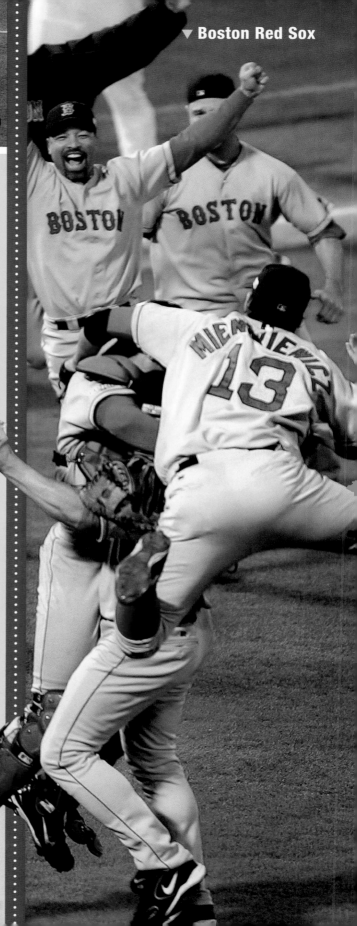

# CHAPTER 4

# POSTSEASON and ALL-STARS

▼ **Boston Red Sox**

The Red Sox found themselves at the brink of elimination in the 2004 American League Championship Series. The New York Yankees had won the first three games, and no team in MLB history had come back after being down 0-3. New York was ahead 4-3 in the ninth inning of Game 4, when the Red Sox rallied against Yankees closer Mariano Rivera. They took Game 4, and went on to win the next three games and the ALCS. The Red Sox rode their momentum to a World Series win, sweeping the St. Louis Cardinals in four games, and ending an 86-year championship drought.

Since the modern era started in 1903, the World Series has pitted the best teams from the American League and National League against each other. Teams battle through the 162-game season for a spot in the playoffs. The St. Louis Cardinals added an 11th championship to their franchise history in 2011, but they have a long way to go to catch the Yankees.

▼ New York Yankees

## MOST WORLD SERIES WINS ||||||| (TEAM)

| | | |
|---|---|---|
| 1. | New York Yankees | 27 |
| 2. | St. Louis Cardinals | 11 |
| 3. | Oakland Athletics | 9 |
| 4. | Boston Red Sox | 7 |
| 5. | Los Angeles Dodgers | 6 |
| | San Francisco Giants | 6 |
| 7. | Cincinnati Reds | 5 |
| | Pittsburgh Pirates | 5 |
| 9. | Detroit Tigers | 4 |
| 10. | Four teams tied with | 3 |

**RECORD FACT** The players with eight or more World Series wins earned all of their championship rings with the New York Yankees.

## MOST WORLD SERIES |||||||||||||| CHAMPIONSHIPS (PLAYER)

| | | |
|---|---|---|
| 1. | Yogi Berra | 10 |
| 2. | Joe DiMaggio | 9 |
| 3. | Bill Dickey | 8 |
| | Phil Rizzuto | 8 |
| | Frankie Crosetti | 8 |
| | Lou Gehrig | 8 |
| 7. | Six players tied with | 7 |

**RECORD FACT** Only three players have won the World Series MVP twice. They are Sandy Koufax, Bob Gibson, and Reggie Jackson.

▲ Yogi Berra

▲ Joe Carter

Hitting a home run to win the World Series is the dream of any player to pick up a baseball. But it has only happened twice in MLB history. Joe Carter of the Toronto Blue Jays came to the plate with his team trailing by one during Game 6 of the 1993 World Series. With two on and one out, he hit a series-winning homer to give the Jays their second straight championship. The only walk-off home run in Game 7 of the World Series belongs to Bill Mazeroski of the 1960 Pittsburgh Pirates. The Pirates second baseman led off the bottom of the ninth inning with the game tied 9-9. He drove the second pitch over the left-field wall, and the Pirates celebrated an upset over the New York Yankees.

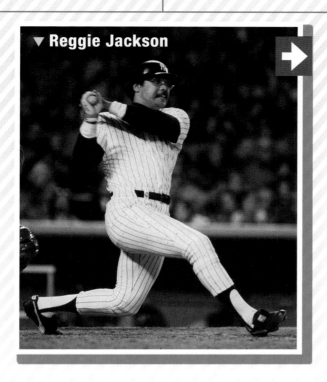
▼ Reggie Jackson

There is a good reason why Reggie Jackson is called Mr. October. He is known for his clutch hitting during the postseason, which helped him to five championship victories. His best performance was in Game 6 of the 1977 World Series. The New York Yankees led the series 3–2 against the Los Angeles Dodgers. Jackson hit home runs in three consecutive at bats, and the Yankees clinched the game and the series. His five home runs in the 1977 World Series have only been matched once. Philadelphia Phillies second baseman Chase Utley hit five homers in the 2009 World Series, but his Phillies still lost to the Yankees.

## ALL STAR APPEARANCES

| | | |
|---|---|---|
| 1. | Hank Aaron | 21 |
| 2. | Willie Mays | 20 |
| | Stan Musial | 20 |
| 4. | Cal Ripken Jr. | 19 |
| 5. | Rod Carew | 18 |
| | Carl Yastrzemski | 18 |
| 7. | Ted Williams | 17 |
| | Pete Rose | 17 |
| 9. | Mickey Mantle | 16 |
| 10. | Five players tied with | 15 |

## ALL-STAR MVPS

Considering the All-Star Game features the best players in baseball, it's quite an honor to be chosen as the All-Star MVP. The award goes to the top player of the game. Only four players have earned the award twice in their careers: Willie Mays, Steve Garvey, Gary Carter, and Cal Ripken Jr.

▲ Willie Mays

▼ Joe DiMaggio

# CHAPTER 5

# BALLPARK FAVORITES

Professional baseball is full of stats, records, and numbers. Sometimes the record is so amazing— or bizarre—that it holds a special place in baseball history.

Although many baseball records are impressive, there are some that are considered unbreakable. Whether the records were made through chance, determination, or a change in the way the game is played, they are considered near impossible to break. Joe DiMaggio's hitting streak is considered one of the unbreakable records in baseball. No player has come within 10 games of DiMaggio's record.

Like Joe DiMaggio, there are other players whose names have become famous for their incredible records. And although any record can be broken, a few may stand the test of time.

▲ Cal Ripken Jr.

### ▼ Cal Ripken Jr.'s Iron Man Streak

Cal Ripken Jr. took the field for a game against the Toronto Blue Jays May 30, 1982. Little did he know that the game would mark the beginning of a legendary streak. Starting with that game, Ripken played in 2,632 consecutive games spanning 17 seasons. He far surpassed Lou Gehrig's 59-year-old record of 2,130 games.

*Why the record will be tough to break:*
Players today rarely play every game in a season. Managers give their players off days to rest. On those days the players still wear their uniforms and watch the game from the dugout, but usually don't play.

### ▼ Cy Young's 511 Wins

You know you've had an impressive career when an award is named after you, and Cy Young is no exception. His most amazing stat is the 511 wins he earned during his career (1890–1911). He started a record 815 games and completed 749 of them—another record.

▼ Cy Young

*Why the record will be tough to break:*
Pitchers today are not expected to pitch in as many games or work through as many innings as pitchers did in Cy Young's era. When starting rotations became popular, pitchers were only expected to start every fourth or fifth game. That gave them fewer chances to earn wins. Plus, relief pitchers often take the reins late in games. The pitchers to come closest to Young's record within the last decade are Greg Maddux and Roger Clemens. They had 355 and 354 wins—not even close to Young's 511.

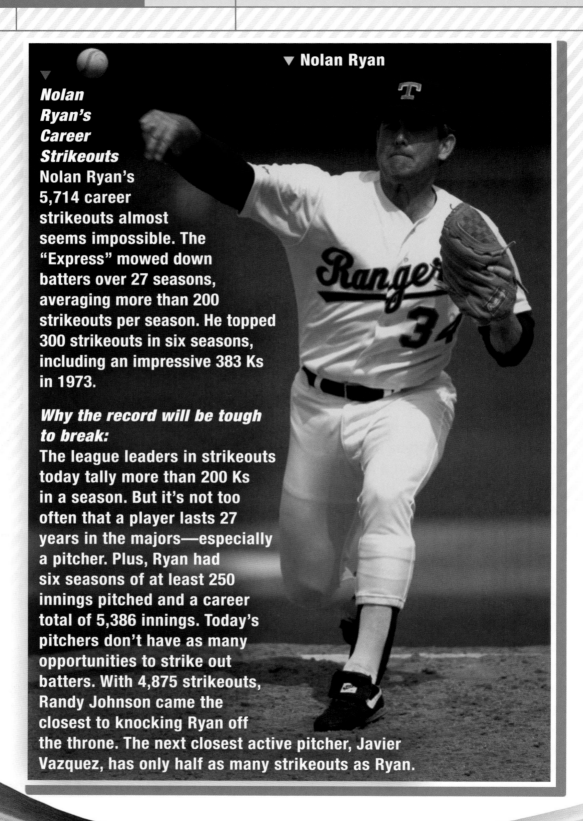

▼ Nolan Ryan

## Nolan Ryan's Career Strikeouts

Nolan Ryan's 5,714 career strikeouts almost seems impossible. The "Express" mowed down batters over 27 seasons, averaging more than 200 strikeouts per season. He topped 300 strikeouts in six seasons, including an impressive 383 Ks in 1973.

### Why the record will be tough to break:

The league leaders in strikeouts today tally more than 200 Ks in a season. But it's not too often that a player lasts 27 years in the majors—especially a pitcher. Plus, Ryan had six seasons of at least 250 innings pitched and a career total of 5,386 innings. Today's pitchers don't have as many opportunities to strike out batters. With 4,875 strikeouts, Randy Johnson came the closest to knocking Ryan off the throne. The next closest active pitcher, Javier Vazquez, has only half as many strikeouts as Ryan.

▼ Johnny Vander Meer

## ▼ *Johnny Vander Meer's Back-to-Back No-Hitters*

Cincinnati Reds pitcher Johnny Vander Meer wasted no time in jumping into the major league spotlight. In 1938, his first full season in the majors, he threw back-to-back no-hitters. He walked three and struck out four in the first game against the Boston Braves. The next game, which was against the Brooklyn Dodgers, was a little wild, with Vander Meer walking eight batters. Despite his lack of control, he didn't allow a single hit, and he remains the only pitcher to achieve the feat.

### *Why the record will be tough to break:*

There have been more than 250 no-hitters in MLB history, so it's possible that a pitcher could repeat the record with back-to-back no-hitters. But to *break* the record, a pitcher would have to throw three straight no-hitters. Nolan Ryan had seven career no-hitters, but the closest two were two months apart.

▼ Alfonso Soriano

### ▼ The 40/40 Club

A player has to have power behind his swing to hit 40 home runs in a season. Similarly, a player needs to be quick on his feet to achieve 40 stolen bases. But it takes an unusual player to hit 40 home runs and steal 40 bases in one season. This elite 40/40 club is made up of only four players: Jose Canseco (1988), Barry Bonds (1996), Alex Rodriguez (1998), and Alfonso Soriano (2006). Amazingly, Soriano also had 41 doubles in 2006.

### ▼ Triple Crown

The triple crown is one of the rarest feats in baseball. Last achieved in 1967, the triple crown is awarded when a player leads or ties his league in home runs, RBIs, and batting average at the end of the season. Thirteen players have won the award. Hall of Famers Ted Williams and Rogers Hornsby accomplished the feat twice.

On the other side of the ball, there's also a triple crown for pitching. It's achieved if a pitcher ties or leads his league in wins, strikeouts, and earned run average at the end of the season. Three players have earned the triple crown three times: Walter Johnson of the Washington Senators, Grover Alexander of the Philadelphia Phillies and the Chicago Cubs, and Sandy Koufax of the Los Angeles Dodgers. In 2011 the Dodgers' Clayton Kershaw earned the National League pitching triple crown. Not to be outdone, the Detroit Tigers' Justin Verlander won the pitching triple crown in the American League.

### The Cycle

If a player gets a single, double, triple, and home run in one game, it's called hitting for the cycle. More than 250 players have hit for the cycle. But only 14 have completed a natural cycle, which is collecting the hits in order (single, double, triple, home run). On May 7, 2008, Carlos Gomez of the Minnesota Twins became the fourth player to hit for the reverse natural cycle (home run, triple, double, single).

▼ **Carlos Gomez**

▼ **Clayton Kershaw**

### Unassisted Triple Plays

A team can get out of a jam quickly if they can turn a triple play. On a rare occasion, it takes only one player to pull it off! Fifteen players have been at the right place at the right time and collected all three outs in a single play. It often happens on a hit-and-run, so the runners are on the move during the pitch. The batter hits a line drive up the middle, and either the second baseman or shortstop snags the ball in the air for the first out. Then he steps on second base for the force out and tags the runner heading to first for the third out. The Detroit Tigers' Johnny Neun and Philadelphia Phillies' Eric Bruntlett are the only players who have ended a game with a triple put out.

# GOLD GLOVE LEADERS

Have you heard the expression that defense wins games? The players on the following lists took that advice to heart.

They were exceptional at their positions and earned many Gold Glove awards during their careers.

 **CATCHER** ||||||||||||||||||||||||||

| | | |
|---|---|---|
| 1. | Ivan Rodriguez | 13 |
| 2. | Johnny Bench | 10 |
| 3. | Bob Boone | 7 |
| 4. | Jim Sundberg | 6 |
| 5. | Bill Freehan | 5 |
| 6. | Del Crandall | 4 |
| | Charles Johnson | 4 |
| | Mike Matheny | 4 |
| | Yadier Molina | 4* |
| | Tony Pena | 4 |

*Active player

▲ Ivan Rodriguez

**PITCHER** ||||||||||||||||||||||||||

| | | |
|---|---|---|
| 1. | Greg Maddux | 18 |
| 2. | Jim Kaat | 16 |
| 3. | Bob Gibson | 9 |
| 4. | Bobby Shantz | 8 |
| 5. | Mark Langston | 7 |
| | Mike Mussina | 7 |
| 7. | Ron Guidry | 5 |
| | Phil Niekro | 5 |
| | Kenny Rogers | 5 |
| 10. | Jim Palmer | 4 |

▲ Greg Maddux

# GOLD GLOVE LEADERS

## FIRST BASE ||||||||||||||||||||||||||

| 1. | Keith Hernandez | 11 |
|----|----|----|
| 2. | Don Mattingly | 9 |
| 3. | George Scott | 8 |
| 4. | Vic Power | 7 |
|    | Bill White | 7 |
| 6. | Wes Parker | 6 |
|    | J.T. Snow | 6 |
| 8. | Steve Garvey | 4 |
|    | Mark Grace | 4 |
|    | Mark Teixeira | 4* |

*Active player

▲ Keith Hernandez

## SECOND BASE ||||||||||||||||||||||||||

| 1. | Roberto Alomar | 10 |
|----|----|----|
| 2. | Ryne Sandberg | 9 |
| 3. | Bill Mazeroski | 8 |
|    | Frank White | 8 |
| 5. | Joe Morgann | 5 |
|    | Bobby Richardson | 5 |
| 7. | Craig Biggio | 4 |
|    | Bret Boone | 4 |
|    | Bobby Grich | 4 |
|    | Orlando Hudson | 4* |

*Active player

▲ Roberto Alomar

# GOLD GLOVE LEADERS

## SHORTSTOP

| | | |
|---|---|---|
| 1. | Ozzie Smith | 13 |
| 2. | Omar Vizquel | 11 |
| 3. | Luis Aparicio | 9 |
| 4. | Mark Belanger | 8 |
| 5. | Dave Concepcion | 5 |
| | Derek Jeter | 5* |
| 7. | Tony Fernandez | 4 |
| | Alan Trammell | 4 |
| 9. | Barry Larkin | 3 |
| | Roy McMillan | 3 |
| | Rey Ordonez | 3 |
| | Jimmy Rollins | 3* |

*Active player

▲ Ozzie Smith

## THIRD BASE

| | | |
|---|---|---|
| 1. | Brooks Robinson | 16 |
| 2. | Mike Schmidt | 10 |
| 3. | Scott Rolen | 8 |
| 4. | Buddy Bell | 6 |
| | Eric Chavez | 6 |
| | Robin Ventura | 6 |
| 7. | Ken Boyer | 5 |
| | Doug Rader | 5 |
| | Ron Santo | 5 |
| 10. | Gary Gaetti | 4 |
| | Matt Williams | 4 |

▲ Brooks Robinson

# GOLD GLOVE LEADERS

| OUTFIELD ||||||||||||||||||||||| | |
|---|---|---|
| 1. | Roberto Clemente | 12 |
| | Willie Mays | 12 |
| 3. | Ken Griffey Jr. | 10 |
| | Andruw Jones | 10* |
| | Al Kaline | 10 |
| | Ichiro Suzuki | 10* |
| 7. | Torii Hunter | 9* |
| 8. | Paul Blair | 8 |
| | Barry Bonds | 8 |
| | Andre Dawson | 8 |
| | Jim Edmonds | 8 |
| | Dwight Evans | 8 |
| | Garry Maddox | 8 |

*Active player

## RECORD FACT

Each season MLB awards the title of Most Valuable Player to one player in the National League and one in the American League. Barry Bonds earned the award seven times in his career—four more than the next closest player.

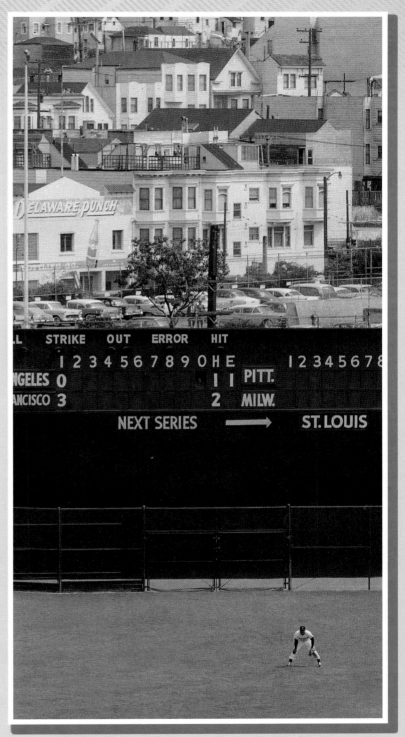

▲ Willie Mays during the Giants' first game in San Francisco after moving from New York in 1958

▼ Tommy John

## MOST SEASONS PLAYED ||||||||||||||||||||||||||||||

| | | | | |
|---|---|---|---|---|
| 1. | Nolan Ryan | 27 | Mets/Angels/Astros/Rangers | 1966, 1968–1993 |
| | Cap Anson | 27 | Forest Cities/Athletics/White Stockings/Colts | 1871–1897 |
| 3. | Deacon McGuire | 26 | Blue Stockings/Wolverines/Quakers/Blues/Broncos/Statesmen/Senators/Superbas/Tigers/Highlanders/Americans/Naps | 1884–1888, 1890–1908, 1910, 1912 |
| | Tommy John | 26 | Indians/White Sox/Dodgers/Yankees/Angels/Athletics | 1963–1974, 1976–1989 |
| 5. | Eddie Collins | 25 | Athletics/White Sox | 1906–1930 |
| | Rickey Henderson | 25 | Athletics/Yankees/Blue Jays/Padres/Angels/Mets/Mariners/Red Sox/Dodgers | 1979–2003 |
| | Charlie Hough | 25 | Dodgers/Rangers/White Sox/Marlins | 1970–1994 |
| | Jim Kaat | 25 | Senators/Twins/White Sox/Phillies/Yankees/Cardinals | 1959–1983 |
| | Bobby Wallace | 25 | Spiders/Perfectos/Browns/Cardinals | 1894–1918 |
| 10. | Many players tied with | 24 | | |

## A FIVE-DECADE RECORD

▼ Minnie Minoso

Minnie Minoso tied a major league record by playing in five decades. He started with the Indians in 1949 at age 23. He played from 1951 through 1964 for four teams, leading the league in triples twice and tying for the lead once. After a 12-year break, he returned to the White Sox for three games in 1976. In 1980, at age 54, he batted twice for the White Sox before ending his career.

Nick Altrock, who set the five-decade record, also played for the White Sox, pitching two complete games for the victorious Sox in the 1906 World Series. He joined the majors in 1898 and made his final plate appearance in 1933 for the Washington Senators, where he had been a coach since 1912.

## RECORD FACT

Youngest Player: Ninth grader Joe Nuxhall pitched for the Cincinnati Reds in a 1944 game when he was 15 years, 10 months, 11 days old.

Oldest Player: Hall of Famer Satchel Paige pitched his last game in 1965 for the Kansas City Athletics when he was 59 years, 2 months, 18 days old.

## LUCKY 13?

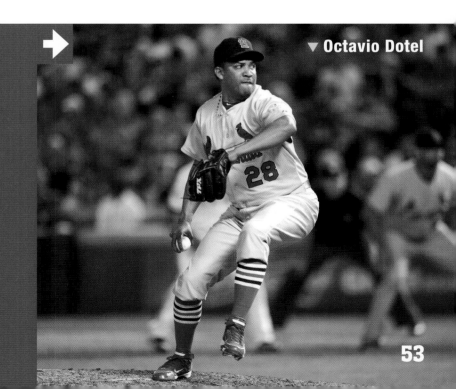
▼ Octavio Dotel

Some players stay with the same team for their entire careers. Other players find themselves in a new uniform every other season. Four players have spent time with 12 teams over their careers: Octavio Dotel, Mike Morgan, Matt Stairs, and Ron Villone. In 2012 Dotel set a record by playing for his 13th team, the Detroit Tigers.

## CAREER WINS BY A MANAGER ||||||||||||||||||||||||||||

| | | | | |
|---|---|---|---|---|
| 1. | Connie Mack | 3,731 | Pirates/Athletics | 1894–1896, 1901–1950 |
| 2. | John McGraw | 2,763 | Orioles/Giants | 1899, 1901–1932 |
| 3. | Tony LaRussa | 2,728 | White Sox/Athletics/Cardinals | 1979–2011 |
| 4. | Bobby Cox | 2,504 | Braves/Blue Jays | 1978–1985, 1990–2010 |
| 5. | Joe Torre | 2,326 | Mets/Braves/Cardinals/Yankees/Dodgers | 1977–1984, 1990–2010 |
| 6. | Sparky Anderson | 2,194 | Reds/Tigers | 1970–1995 |
| 7. | Bucky Harris | 2,158 | Senators/Tigers/Red Sox/Phillies/Yankees | 1924–1943, 1947–1948, 1950–1956 |
| 8. | Joe McCarthy | 2,125 | Cubs/Yankees/Red Sox | 1926–1946, 1948–1950 |
| 9. | Walter Alston | 2,040 | Dodgers | 1954–1976 |
| 10. | Leo Durocher | 2,008 | Dodgers/Giants/Cubs/Astros | 1939–1946, 1948–1955, 1966–1973 |

## WIN SOME, LOSE SOME

Connie Mack tops the wins list, but he also tops the list of all-time losses by a manager with 3,948. Next in line is Tony LaRussa, but he has about 1,500 fewer losses than Mack.

And speaking of winners, Casey Stengel led the New York Yankees to five straight World Series victories from 1949 to 1953.

▼ Connie Mack

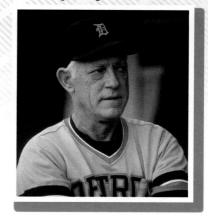

▼ Sparky Anderson

| WORLD SERIES CHAMPIONSHIPS BY A MANAGER ‖‖‖‖‖ | | | |
|---|---|---|---|
| 1. | Joe McCarthy | 7 | Cubs/Yankees/Red Sox | 1926–1946, 1948–1950 |
| | Casey Stengel | 7 | Dodgers/Bees/ Braves/Yankees/Mets | 1934–1936, 1938–1943, 1949–1960, 1962–1965 |
| 3. | Connie Mack | 5 | Pirates/Athletics | 1894–1896, 1901–1950 |
| 4. | Walter Alston | 4 | Dodgers | 1954–1976 |
| | Joe Torre | 4 | Mets/Braves/ Cardinals/Yankees/ Dodgers | 1977–1984, 1990–2010 |
| 6. | Sparky Anderson | 3 | Reds/Tigers | 1970–1995 |
| | Miller Huggins | 3 | Cardinals/Yankees | 1913–1929 |
| | Tony LaRussa | 3 | White Sox/Athletics/ Cardinals | 1979–2011 |
| | John McGraw | 3 | Orioles/Giants | 1899, 1901–1932 |
| 10. | Many managers tied with | 2 | | |

## RECORD FACT

Bobby Cox of the Atlanta Braves is the only manager to get ejected twice in the World Series. The first happened in 1992 during an argument over a check swing call. The second happened in 1996 when he disagreed with a called out of a baserunner attempting to steal.

# THE BEST OF THE WORST

Some players earn records they'd rather not have. They can only hope that another player will come along who will take the title of "the best of the worst."

▼ Jim Thome

| | | CAREER STRIKEOUTS | | |
|---|---|---|---|---|
| 1. | Reggie Jackson | 2,597 | Athletics/Orioles/Yankees/Angels | 1967–1987 |
| 2. | Jim Thome | 2,487 | Indians/Phillies/White Sox/Dodgers/Twins | 1991–2011* |
| 3. | Sammy Sosa | 2,306 | Rangers/White Sox/Cubs/Orioles | 1989–2005, 2007 |
| 4. | Andres Galarraga | 2,003 | Expos/Cardinals/Rockies/Braves/Rangers/Giants/Expos/Angels | 1985–1998, 2000–2004 |
| 5. | Jose Canseco | 1,942 | Athletics/Rangers/Red Sox/Blue Jays/Devil Rays/Yankees/White Sox | 1985–2001 |
| 6. | Willie Stargell | 1,936 | Pirates | 1962–1982 |
| 7. | Alex Rodriguez | 1,916 | Mariners/Rangers/Yankees | 1994–2011* |
| 8. | Mike Cameron | 1,901 | White Sox/Reds/Mariners/Mets/Padres/Brewers/Red Sox/Marlins | 1995–2011* |
| 9. | Mike Schmidt | 1,883 | Phillies | 1972–1989 |
| 10. | Fred McGriff | 1,882 | Blue Jays/Padres/Braves/Devil Rays/Cubs/Dodgers | 1986–2004 |

*Active player

# THE BEST OF THE WORST

## SINGLE SEASON STRIKEOUTS ||||||||||||||||||||||||||

| | | | | |
|---|---|---|---|---|
| 1. | **Mark Reynolds** | 223 | Diamondbacks | 2009 |
| 2. | **Mark Reynolds** | 211 | Diamondbacks | 2010 |
| 3. | **Drew Stubbs** | 205 | Reds | 2011 |
| 4. | **Mark Reynolds** | 204 | Diamondbacks | 2008 |
| 5. | **Adam Dunn** | 199 | Nationals | 2010 |
| | **Ryan Howard** | 199 | Phillies | 2007 |
| | **Ryan Howard** | 199 | Phillies | 2008 |
| 8. | **Jack Cust** | 197 | Athletics | 2008 |
| 9. | **Mark Reynolds** | 196 | Orioles | 2011 |
| 10. | **Adam Dunn** | 195 | Reds | 2004 |

**RECORD FACT** Eight players have struck out six times in one game. Alex Gonzalez of the Toronto Blue Jays is the only one of them to strike out during every plate appearance.

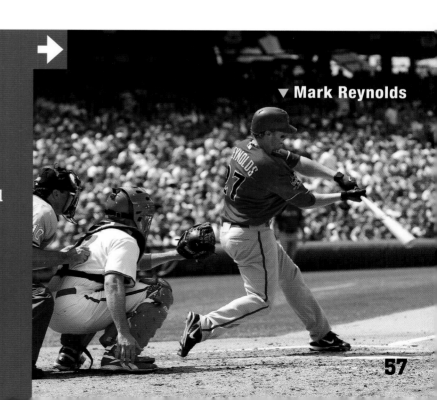

## SWINGING FOR THE FENCES

In only five years in the majors, Mark Reynolds has hit 158 home runs, averaging about 32 per season. But with the big swings come big misses. In four of his five seasons, Reynolds has landed in the top 10 for single-season strikeouts. With 963 strikeouts through 2011, Reynolds may find himself in the top 10 career strikeouts list before long.

▼ Mark Reynolds

# THE BEST OF THE WORST

| # | Name | Errors | Teams | Years |
|---|------|--------|-------|-------|
| 1. | Herman Long | 1,096 | Cowboys/Beaneaters/Highlanders/Tigers/Phillies | 1889–1904 |
| 2. | Bill Dahlen | 1,080 | Colts/Orphans/Superbas/Giants/Doves/Dodgers | 1891–1911 |
| 3. | Deacon White | 1,018 | Forest Citys/Red Stockings/White Stockings/Reds/Bisons/Wolverines/Alleghenys | 1871–1890 |
| 4. | Germany Smith | 1,009 | Mountain City/Blues/Grays/Reds/Bridegrooms/Browns | 1884–1898 |
| 5. | Tommy Corcoran | 992 | Burghers/Athletics/Grooms/Bridegrooms/Reds/Giants | 1890–1907 |
| 6. | Fred Pfeffer | 980 | Trojans/White Stockings/Pirates/Colonels/Giants/Colts | 1882–1897 |
| 7. | Cap Anson | 976 | Forest Citys/Athletics/White Stockings/Colts | 1871–1897 |
| 8. | Monte Ward | 952 | Grays/Gothams/Giants/Ward's Wonders/Grooms | 1878–1894 |
| 9. | Jack Glasscock | 895 | Blues/Outlaw Reds/Maroons/Hoosiers/Giants/Browns/Pirates/Colonels/Senators | 1879–1895 |
| 10. | Ed McKean | 892 | Blues/Spiders/Perfectos | 1887–1899 |

## ERROR UPON ERROR

In 1889 Herman Long of the Kansas City Cowboys committed 122 errors in 137 games. The Philadelphia Athletics' Billy Shindle was even worse in 1890 if you consider the number of games played. He committed 122 errors in 132 games. Andy Leonard of the Boston Red Stockings didn't have many career errors, but he had one of the worst outings of any fielder in MLB history. He committed nine errors during one game in 1876!

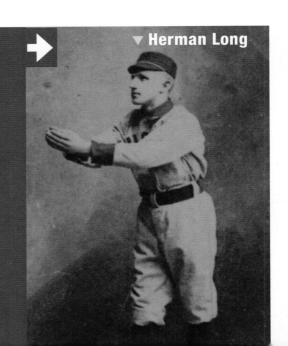

► Herman Long

# THE BEST OF THE WORST

## CAREER HIT BATTERS

| | | | | |
|---|---|---|---|---|
| 1. | Gus Weyhing | 277 | Athletics/Ward's Wonders/Phillies/Pirates/Colonels/Senators/Cardinals/Superbas/Reds/Blues | 1887–1896, 1898–1901 |
| 2. | Chick Fraser | 219 | Colonels/Spiders/Phillies/Athletics/Beaneaters/Reds/Cubs | 1896–1909 |
| 3. | Pink Hawley | 210 | Browns/Pirates/Reds/Giants/Brewers | 1892–1901 |
| 4. | Walter Johnson | 205 | Senators | 1907–1927 |
| 5. | Randy Johnson | 190 | Expos/Mariners/Astros/Diamondbacks/Yankees/Giants | 1988–2009 |
| | Eddie Plank | 190 | Athletics/Terriers/Browns | 1901–1917 |
| 7. | Tim Wakefield | 186 | Pirates/Red Sox | 1992–1993, 1995–2011 |
| 8. | Tony Mullane | 185 | Wolverines/Eclipse/Browns/Blue Stockings/Red Stockings/Orioles/Spiders | 1881–1884, 1886–1894 |
| 9. | Joe McGinnity | 179 | Orioles/Superbas/Giants | 1899–1908 |
| 10. | Charlie Hough | 174 | Dodgers/Rangers/White Sox/Marlins | 1970–1994 |

**RECORD FACT** It's no wonder Tim Wakefield is in the top 10 for career hit batters. Wakefield is well-known for his knuckleball, a pitch with movement that is tough to predict—for the hitter, pitcher, *and* catcher.

## BACK-TO-BACK-TO-BACK-TO-BACK

▼ Dave Bush

Only three pitchers have given up four home runs in a row. The Los Angeles Angels' Paul Foytack gave up four consecutive bombs against the Cleveland Indians in 1963. New York Yankees pitcher Chase Wright suffered the same fate in 2007 at the hands of the rival Boston Red Sox. Dave Bush of the Milwaukee Brewers was taken deep four times in a row by the Arizona Diamondbacks in 2010. Teams have hit four straight home runs on four other occasions, but they were against multiple pitchers.

# WILD PITCHES

▼ **Tony Mullane**

## CAREER

| | | | | |
|---|---|---|---|---|
| 1. | **Tony Mullane** | 343 | Wolverines/Eclipse/ Browns/Blue Stockings/Red Stockings/Orioles/ Spiders | 1881–1884, 1886–1894 |
| 2. | **Nolan Ryan** | 277 | Mets/Angels/Astros/ Rangers | 1966, 1968–1993 |
| 3. | **Mickey Welch** | 274 | Trojans/Gothams/ Giants | 1881–1892 |
| 4. | **Bobby Mathews** | 253 | Kekiongas/Canaries/ Mutuals/Reds/Grays/ Red Stockings/ Athletics | 1871–1877, 1879, 1881–1887 |
| 5. | **Tim Keefe** | 240 | Trojans/ Metropolitans/ Giants/Phillies | 1880–1993 |
| | **Gus Weyhing** | 240 | Athletics/Ward's Wonders/Phillies/ Pirates/Colonels/ Senators/Cardinals/ Superbas/Reds | 1887–1896, 1898–1901 |
| 7. | **Phil Niekro** | 226 | Braves/Yankees/ Indians/Blue Jays | 1965–1987 |
| 8. | **Mark Baldwin** | 221 | White Stockings/ Solons/Pirates/Giants | 1887–1893 |
| | **Pud Galvin** | 221 | Brown Stockings/ Bisons/Alleghenys/ Burghers/Pirates/ Browns | 1875, 1879–1892 |
| | **Will White** | 221 | Red Stockings/Reds/ Wolverines | 1877–1886 |

# WILD PITCHES

| SINGLE SEASON | | | | |
|---|---|---|---|---|
| 1. | Mark Baldwin | 83 | Solons | 1889 |
| 2. | Tony Mullane | 63 | Blue Stockings | 1884 |
| | Bill Stemmyer | 63 | Beaneaters | 1886 |
| 4. | Mike Morrison | 62 | Blues | 1887 |
| 5. | Matt Kilroy | 61 | Orioles | 1886 |
| 6. | Ed Seward | 58 | Athletics | 1887 |
| 7. | Jersey Bakley | 56 | Keystones/Quicksteps/Cowboys | 1884 |
| | Gus Weyhing | 56 | Athletics | 1888 |
| 9. | Ed Seward | 54 | Athletics | 1888 |
| 10. | Tony Mullane | 53 | Red Stockings | 1886 |

▼ J.R. Richard

## REALLY, REALLY WILD

Three pitchers have had six wild pitches in a single game: Phil Niekro of the Atlanta Braves, J.R. Richard of the Houston Astros, and Bill Gullickson of the Montreal Expos. During an 1890 game, Bert Cunningham of the Buffalo Bisons threw five wild pitches in a single inning.

# READ MORE

**Berman, Len**. *The Greatest Moments in Sports*. Naperville, Ill.: Sourcebooks, 2009.

**Fischer, David**. *Babe Ruth: Legendary Slugger*. New York: Sterling Publishing, 2010.

**Jacobs, Greg**. *The Everything Kids' Baseball Book: From Baseball History to Player Stats—With Lots of Homerun Fun in Between!* Avon, Mass.: Adams Media, 2010.

**LeBoutillier, Nate**. *The Best of Everything Baseball Book*. Mankato, Minn.: Capstone Press, 2011.

# INTERNET SITES

FactHound offers a safe, fun way to find Internet sites related to this book. All of the sites on FactHound have been researched by our staff.

Here's all you do:

Visit *www.facthound.com*

**Type in this code: 9781429687140**

# INDEX